Ark Adventures

Noah and his wife think a flood might be coming, so they have built a big boat called the Ark. They are sailing around the world to rescue the animals before it starts to rain.

Let's all go on an animal adventure!

For John Etherington
S.G.

For Martha
A.P.

Reading Consultant: Prue Goodwin, Lecturer in literacy and children's books

ORCHARD BOOKS
338 Euston Road, London NW1 3BH
Orchard Books Australia
Level 17/207 Kent Street, Sydney, NSW 2000

First published in 2011
First paperback publication in 2012

ISBN 978 1 40830 555 3 (hardback)
ISBN 978 1 40830 563 8 (paperback)

A CIP catalogue record for this book is available from the British Library.

1 3 5 7 9 10 8 6 4 2 (hardback)
1 3 5 7 9 10 8 6 4 2 (paperback)

Printed in China

Orchard Books is a division of Hachette Children's Books,
an Hachette UK company.

Giant
Giraffes!

Written by Sally Grindley

Illustrated by Alex Paterson

ORCHARD BOOKS

"Look at the sign," Noah said to
his wife one morning. "We've
reached Africa!"
"I've always wanted to go to Africa,"
said Mrs Noah. "Which animals
will we find there?"

Noah opened their *Big Book of Animals.*

"Elephants, lions, zebras, hippos,

giraffes and lots more," said Noah.

"Let's find the giraffes first," said
Mrs Noah. "I like the word *giraffe*."
"It says they're *always* hungry and
very tall," said Noah.

"I hope they'll fit on the Ark!" said
Mrs Noah.
They went to put on their safari
clothes.

Soon they were sailing up a <u>wide</u>
river. Suddenly Noah cried, "Stop!
I saw something!"
Mrs Noah stopped the Ark.
"There, behind that tree," said Noah.

"Would you mind standing up
straight, so that we can see you?"
Noah called out.

A long neck stretched upwards.

Two large eyes blinked at them.

"Look at that, Mrs Noah," exclaimed
Noah. "He's almost as tall as
the tree!"
"What beautiful eyes!" said
Mrs Noah. "And what a pretty
patchwork coat!"

The giraffe began to move away.

"Don't go!" cried Noah.

"We'll have to be quick to catch up
with him," said Mrs Noah.

"I know. Let's use the stilts!"

"Good idea!" said Noah. He went to

find them.

"Now I will feel like a giraffe!"

Noah said.

"Well, you *are* always hungry," said

Mrs Noah. "Take this bag of onions.

Our book says giraffes like them."

Noah set off with the stilts and the

bag of onions on his back.

Noah put the stilts against a tree.

He climbed the tree, then lowered

himself onto them.

"Whoa!" he cried. "I'm *very* tall."

"Hurry, Noah!" shouted Mrs Noah.

"There are two giraffes now."

Noah set off, wobbling this way . . .

. . . wobbling that way.

"Wait for me," he called to the giraffes. "I've got a treat for you!"

The giraffes twitched their noses.

"I knew it!" said Noah. "You're

hungry!"

One of the giraffes stuck its tongue

into the bag on Noah's back.

"That's it!" said Noah. "Now,

follow me."

He began to walk back to the
Ark, wobbling this way . . .

. . . wobbling that way.

The giraffes followed him!
When Mrs Noah saw them she clapped
her hands. "You *are* clever, Noah."

The giraffes followed Noah up the gangplank. But when they reached the top, they couldn't go any further. The door to the Ark was too low!

"Try bending over," said Noah.

He bent his neck to show them how.

But the giraffes still couldn't fit

through the door!

"Wait there," said Noah.

Noah went to get a saw. He sawed
the doorway to make it higher. The
giraffes walked through the doorway.
But inside, the ceiling was too low!
"Wait there," said Noah.